Cluck Cluck Duck

This first edition was printed by
Printout Colour Printers Ltd. www.printout-uk.com

Derek Duck woke up as the sun streamed through the window of his humble houseboat.

Throwing back his cosy quilt he bounced out of bed.

He quickly washed and wrapped himself in his favourite red coat and waddled outside to celebrate…

HIS BIRTHDAY!

He raised a wing to wave at his friends. The circus frogs, the snorkelling newts, the racing water boatmen, the living statue heron and above it all the iridescent dragonflies twirling and spinning like disco lights.

Today, to Derek's surprise, there was no one there. He quacked a call across the water but there was no reply. Shrugging, he set off to his favourite field.

He waddled up the steep slope and pushed the gate open but the only sound was the buzzing of bees bouncing on buttercups.

Confused, he waddled towards the sheep field.

He pushed the wooden gate open but all he saw was grass. It felt eerie. This field was always noisy. Derek began to worry.

He ran to the next field hoping to find anyone.

He opened the big gate but before he had time to think, he heard a roar…

"SURPRISE!
HAPPY BIRTHDAY!"

Derek opened his beak to quack a scream but to everyone's amazement he shouted....

"CLUCK! CLUCK!"

Everyone gasped. Derek quickly clamped his wings over his beak. After a while, and with a little encouragement from his friends, he slowly unwrapped his wings and opened his beak but heard......

"Cluck! Cluck! Cluck!"

Two elf owls huddled together.
They hooted in hushed tones
and soon hatched a plan.

"Derek you have the cluck-ups.
Don't worry, we'll help you.
Try eating some birthday cake
and drinking some juice."

Derek quickly waddled over
to the huge tree stump table.

He happily munched the cake and slurped the juice.

When he was finished he took a deep breath, opened his beak and.....

"Cluck Cluck Cluck!"

The animals winced, the plan didn't work,
but the owls had another idea.

"Derek", they ordered,
"get your present, the
big red trampoline.
Yes that's it.

Now bounce and
back flip… oh and
hold your breath."

All the animals cheered
as they watched Derek
bounce up and over,
down and up.

He stopped after ten jumps
and opened his beak to hear....

"Cluck
cluck
cluck
cluck
cluck!"

The elf owls quickly thought of another idea,
"Derek, let's all go to the pond. Come on let's go!"

Most of the animals followed the little owls down to the pond...

...but nobody noticed a chicken silently slip away from the party.

Everyone was too busy thinking up more ideas to help Derek get his quack back.

The elf owls nervously hooted more instructions, "Derek, try to wing stand while drinking some water from the pond."

Derek scratched his head but couldn't think of a better idea, so he scooped up some water in a cup and tried his best.

When Derek finished his wing stand
he opened his beak and heard...

"Cluck! Cluck!"

All the animals shrugged. There were no more ideas.
So, Derek gave up. He was very tired.

Yawning, he waved goodbye to everyone, walked back
to his houseboat and hung his coat on a little brass hook.

He was about to have a bath when...

CREEEAK!

Spinning around he noticed some squeaking and scuffling noises coming from his bedroom. Something was in there. Derek began to feel very scared.

He tiptoed to his bedroom. He was right. He could hear breathing. He gulped but bravely opened the door. The room was much darker now.

Grabbing a torch he shuffled towards an unusual shape…

…but before he could get too close, a chicken jumped out shouting…

Derek tried to cluck a scream but to his delight
the sound that he heard was a huge….

"Quack!"

He was so happy that he quacked as he jumped out of
his bedroom window. Everyone was there setting up
his party and they all cheered when they heard him.
Derek could finally enjoy celebrating his birthday thanks
to chicken with her surprise plan.

Jean Blakey studied English at Bradford College and has been writing stories since she was a child. She originally used a typewriter perched on a windowsill and as she was outside considered this as an outdoor pursuit. After winning some awards as a teenager Jean decided to use her writing skills to raise funds for charity. This book is her first commercial publication.

Jonathan Nash is an award winning illustrator influenced by the countryside of rural England. Although he lives about as far from the coast as possible in Leicestershire, he loves the seaside, painting a popular series called SeaCat & Pipsqueak. With all of his watercolours, Jonathan wants to make people smile, feel happy and escape to a gentler world (mostly inhabited by humorous and kind animals!).

Don't forget you can contact us by visiting the website: www.cluckcluckduck.uk